This Ladybird Book belongs to:

_____

_____

_____

_____

Retold by Audrey Daly
Illustrated by Chris Russell

Cover illustration by John Gurney

Copyright © Ladybird Books USA 1996

Originally published in the United Kingdom by Ladybird Books Ltd © 1993

First American edition by Ladybird Books USA
An Imprint of Penguin USA Inc.
375 Hudson Street, New York, New York 10014

Printed in Great Britain
10 9 8 7 6 5 4 3 2 1

ISBN 0-7214-5623-5

FAVORITE TALES

Goldilocks and the Three Bears

nce upon time, in a little house in the middle of the forest lived three bears.

There was great big Father Bear, and medium-sized Mother Bear, and little tiny Baby Bear.

Honey

One morning, Mother Bear made a big pot of porridge and put it into three bowls for breakfast.

The porridge smelled delicious, but it was much too hot to eat.

"Let us take a walk in the forest while the porridge cools," said Father Bear. "When we come back, it will be just right." So off they went into the forest.

Nearby there lived a very naughty and mischievous little girl named Goldilocks. She was called Goldilocks because she had long, golden hair.

That morning, as she was passing the three bears' house, Goldilocks saw that the front door was wide open.

"I will just have a little peek inside," she said to herself.

When Goldilocks saw the porridge
she rushed over to taste it.

She tasted the porridge in Father
Bear's bowl, but it was too hot.

Then, she tasted the porridge in Mother Bear's bowl, but it was too lumpy.

Finally, she tasted the porridge in Baby Bear's bowl. It wasn't too hot, and it wasn't too lumpy. It was just right! So Goldilocks ate it all up.

After that, Goldilocks wanted to sit down. She sat in Father Bear's big chair, but it was too high.

She sat in Mother Bear's medium-sized chair. "This is too hard!" she grumbled.

Then she sat in Baby Bear's tiny chair. It wasn't too high. It wasn't too hard. It was just right!

But Goldilocks was much too heavy for
Baby Bear's little chair. With a *creak*
and a *crack*, the chair fell to pieces.

"Ouch!" cried Goldilocks as she
landed in a heap on the floor.
"That hurt!" she said crossly.
"Now I must lie down."

So Goldilocks went upstairs. She tried
Father Bear's big bed, but that was much
too hard.

She tried Mother Bear's medium-sized
bed, but that was much too soft.

Then she tried Baby Bear's tiny bed.
It wasn't too hard. It wasn't too soft.
"This is just right!" she said. Soon she
was fast asleep.

Before long, the three bears came
home from their walk.

"I am hungry!" said Father Bear. But
when he got to the table he cried out
in surprise, "Someone has been
eating my porridge!"

Mother Bear said, "And someone
has been eating my porridge!"

"Someone has been eating my porridge," cried Baby Bear, holding his empty bowl, "and they have eaten it all up!"

"Look!"
said Father Bear.
"Someone has
been sitting
in my
chair!"

"And someone has been sitting in *my* chair," said Mother Bear.

"Someone has been sitting in my chair," cried poor little Baby Bear, "and they have broken it to pieces!"

The three bears began to search the house. Father Bear looked upstairs. "Someone has been sleeping in my bed!" he said.

"And someone has been sleeping in *my* bed," cried Mother Bear.

"Oh!" squeaked Baby Bear. "Someone has been sleeping in my bed and she is *still here!*"

At the sound of Baby Bear's voice,
Goldilocks woke up. The first thing she
saw was Father Bear, looking very angry.

Goldilocks jumped up in fright. She ran down the stairs and out of the house as fast as she could.

"I do not think she will trouble us again," said Father Bear, smiling.

And she never did.

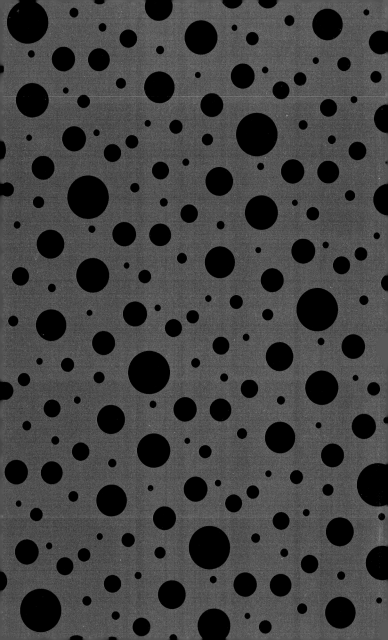